To my parents,
with love and gratitude —H. K.

To Abbas —M. A.

Text © 2012 by Hena Khan.
Illustrations © 2012 by Mehrdokht Amini.

Library of Congress Cataloging-in-Publication Data
Khan, Hena.
Golden domes and silver lanterns : a Muslim book of colors / by Hena Khan : illustrated by Mehrdokht Amini.
p. cm.
Summary: In simple rhyming text a young Muslim girl and her family guide the reader through the traditions and colors of Islam.
ISBN 978-0-8118-7905-7 (alk. paper)
1. Islam–Customs and practices–Juvenile fiction. 2. Muslims–Juvenile fiction. 3. Colors–Juvenile fiction. 4. Stories in rhyme. [1.
Stories in rhyme. 2. Islam–Customs and practices–Fiction. 3. Muslims–Fiction. 4. Color–Fiction.] I. Amini, Mehrdokht, ill. II. Title.
PZ8.3.K493Go 2012
[E]–dc23
2011030672

Book design by Amelia May Mack.
Typeset in Tournedot.

Manufactured in China.

1 3 5 7 9 10 8 6 4 2

Chronicle Books LLC, 680 Second Street, San Francisco, California 94107

www.chroniclekids.com

Golden Domes and Silver Lanterns

A Muslim Book of Colors

by Hena Khan

illustrated by

Mehrdokht Amini

chronicle books · san francisco

Red is the rug
Dad kneels on to pray,
facing toward Mecca,
five times a day.

Blue is the hijab
Mom likes to wear.
It's a scarf she uses to cover her hair.

Gold is the dome of the mosque, big and grand. Beside it two towering minarets stand.

White is a kufi,
round and flat.
Grandpa wears
this traditional hat.

Black is the ink
I use to draw
the Arabic letters
that spell Allah.

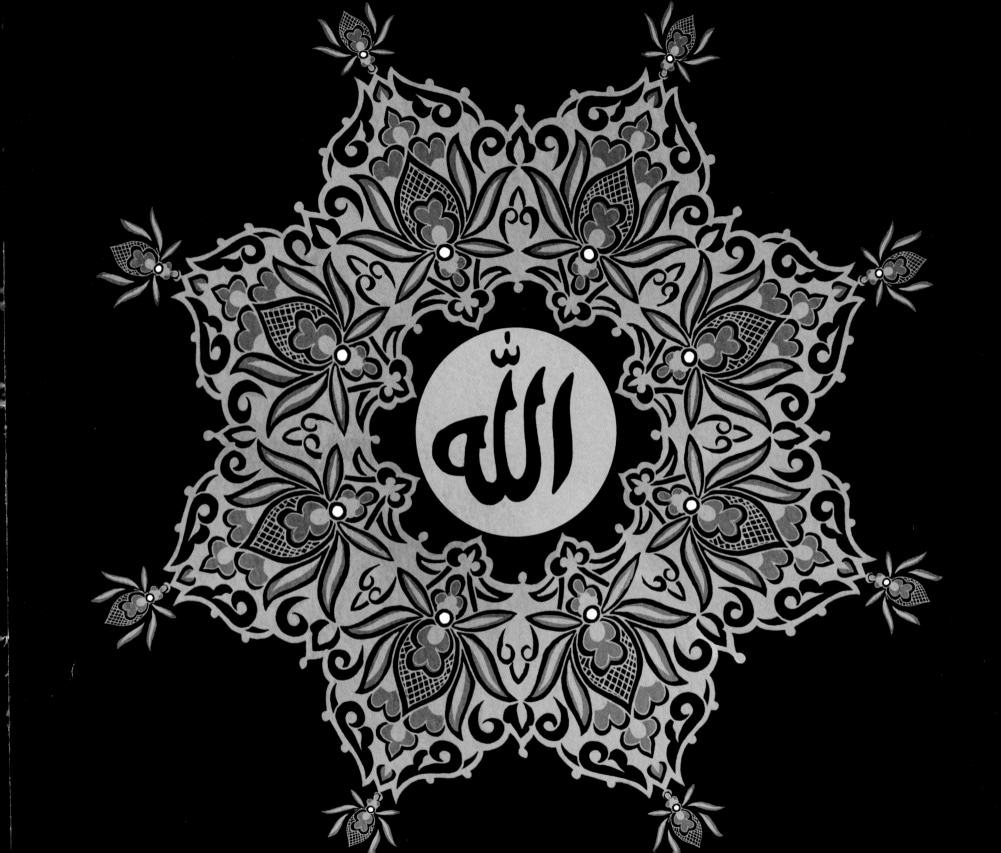

Brown is a date,
plump and sweet.
During Ramadan,
it's my favorite treat.

Orange is the color of my henna designs.
They cover my hands in leafy vines.

Purple is an Eid gift
just for me.
I open it up
and love what I see.

Yellow is the box
we fill on Eid
with gifts of zakat
for those in need.

Green is the **Quran**
I read with pride.
Grandma explains
the lessons inside.

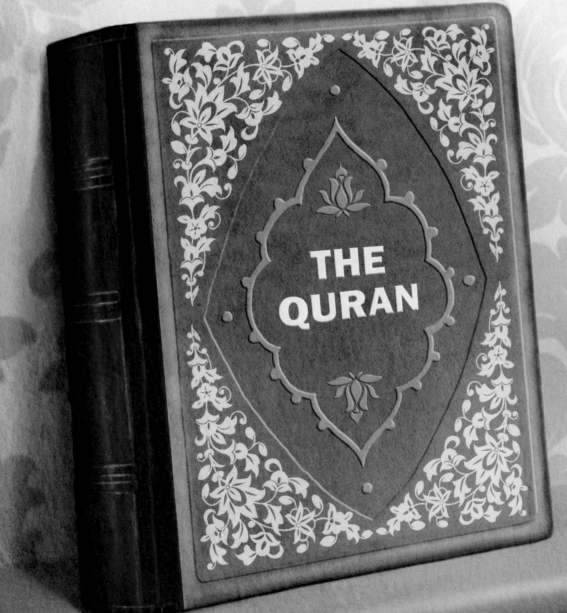

Silver is a fanoos,
a twinkling light,
a shiny lantern
that glows at night.

All of the
colorful things we've seen
make up the world of my faith,
my **deen**.

THE QURAN

ZAKAT زكاة

Glossary

Allah (al-LAH): the Arabic word for "God."

Deen: an Arabic word that translates to "religion" or "way of life."

Eid (EED): an Islamic holiday. There are two Eid holidays. Eid-ul-Fitr marks the end of Ramadan, and Eid-ul-Adha is a celebration of life focusing on sacrifice and devotion to God.

Fanoos (fun-OOSE): a lantern used in the Middle East that is made out of tin and glass. In Middle Eastern countries, fanoos are lit by children in celebration of Ramadan.

Henna: a dye made from dried leaves used to temporarily decorate skin with a dark orange tint. Muslim women from various cultures decorate their hands with henna for celebrations, including Eid and weddings.

Hijab (hih-JAB): the head covering that many Muslim women wear, especially while praying or in public. The word hijab means "curtain" or "cover" in Arabic.

Kufi (KOO-fee): a short, brimless, rounded cap worn by Muslim men and boys from various countries.

Mecca (MEK-ka): a city in Saudi Arabia. It is the most sacred place in Islam. Every day, Muslims all over the world kneel on prayer rugs to pray in the direction of Mecca.

Minaret (min-ah-RET): a tower at a mosque. A "call to prayer" is broadcast from a minaret to let Muslims know it is time to pray.

Mosque (MOSK): a place where Muslims gather to pray together.

Quran (kur-AHN): the holy book of Islam. Muslims are encouraged to memorize portions of the Quran, and to read it with love and devotion.

Ramadan (rahm-uh-DAHN): the ninth month in the Islamic calendar, and the holiest month for Muslims. During Ramadan, Muslims fast from sunrise to sunset each day, and they traditionally break the fast with dates and milk. Muslims also say extra prayers and give to charity during Ramadan.

Zakat (zah-KAT): money given by Muslims to the poor and others in need.